W9-COY-798

Jesse's Color Field

Written & Illustrated by S.K. Miller

Treehouse Treasures

Books for the Heart of a Child

Chapter 1
Birds Can't Talk!

Jesse laid dreaming on an old gray fence beneath the tall timber trees of Color Field. The clouds that rolled slowly overhead seemed to smile and swirl as Jesse spoke to them.

"Hot dog! You're the biggest *bestest* cloud I've ever seen," declared the boy. He smiled and said to himself, "Hoof hop...if I were a horse, I would go plip-pitty plop. But if I were a cloud, I could be a speeding train too, and a tiger, and a rocket ship, and a...and a giant purple frog, or anything!"

"Mr. Cloud, how can you be *so many* different things?" asked the boy. "Sometimes, you're a *giant* horse galloping through the air; and sometimes I see funny faces *laughing* and *cheering*."

The boy paused. With eyes big and bright his voice rang out, "Wow! Look at that train barreling across the sky!"

Just then, Jesse thought he heard the cloud say, "The storm is coming. The stormmm...isss comingggg."

And soon after, another voice squeaked out. "Good day, boy! Chirp!"

Jesse looked all around, but there was no one to be found.

"Well, I'm right here boy...*down* here!" squeaked the voice.

Jesse looked down to his feet to see a little brown bird. "Sufferin' succotash, what's wrong with your eyes boy? *Here* I am," peeped the bird.

"Oh, creepers!" Jesse shouted, falling back on his bottom. "But...but, you're a bird!"

"Of course! What *else* would I be?" squawked the bird.

The boy was puzzled, confused. He rubbed his eyes and looked again. Again, the bird squeaked, "I'm still *here*."

"Yea, and...and still a *bird*!" shouted Jesse. "I thought birds can't talk."

"Can't *talk*?" exclaimed the bird, "That's hogwash! You *can* hear me, can't ya?"

4

"Sure I can," replied the boy, "It's just that... well, I've never talked to a bird before."

The bird squawked, "Snap out of it kid! This is no time to get starry-eyed. My name is Kraukey, and I need your *help*."

"What's wrong?" asked the boy.

The little bird flew over to the fence and quickly fell off. "Whahoo!" yelled Kraukey.

Jesse blurted, "Be careful Mr. Kraukey," while catching the bird in his hands.

"Khuh ha ha....I'm all wobbly after that lightnin' nearly cooked my gizzard," laughed the bird.

"*Lightning*?" Jesse shouted.

"You *betcha,* and *lots* of it," Kraukey replied,
"An *awful* storm is comin'. There's gonna' be nothin' left in Color Field."
"Our homes will be destroyed!" crowed Kraukey.

"Oh, *no*...what can we do?" asked the boy.

"You can tell those cranky clouds to go blow some other way!"
snapped the bird. "After all boy, you're busy blabberin' with them
all day *anyway.* So, *this* should be no trouble at all."

Jesse shook his head and stumbled to say, "But...but, I just
pretend Kraukey. They don't *really* talk to me."

Kraukey cried out, "That's not true! I hear those windbags yappin'
with you every day."

Rather surprised, Jesse asked, "*You* do?"

"Boy, you *must* believe. Without you, we're doomed!" Kraukey shouted.

Jesse leaned back against the fence to think. "But it's all sunny
and...and well, I don't see any storm coming."

"Listen boy, we don't have time for this!" Kraukey insisted,
"I just came from that storm. So, *I* can be quite certain that it's comin'."

6

Kraukey shivered, "...whole trees ripped from the ground! And the lightnin' burned *my* feathers!" wailed the bird.

"That *is* unfortunate," the boy replied.

"Unfortunate? I'll say! They're *my* feathers ya know......the *only* feathers I've got!" yelled Kraukey.

Jesse stood up and declared, "You can count on me Kraukey. I'll help you."

Happily, Kraukey danced around laughing. "Ha ha...now you're talkin' kiddo!"

Without wasting another moment, Jesse and Kraukey began their journey to the highest hilltop of Color Field. There, Jesse would be closest to the clouds. If he was going to convince the storm not to destroy everything, they believed it best to speak with the clouds there.

Chapter 2
Giggles & Grumps

Unbeknownst to Jesse and the little bird, they had been overheard by a sort unlike most friendly critters. Among the grass, young weeds, and old dried out leaves was a tunnel dug deeply into the ground. It lead to the burrow of an old crusty rat, named Rufuss. The rat's guest, Perce Prairie Dog, quietly nibbled on a cookie, sipped her tea, and listened.

"Well, I find it hard to believe that a stranger and a *boy* no less, would be so concerned as to help us. We've never even met this boy," hissed the rat. "He could be just another lazy *oaf*...laying around on that fence all day. Why, he could be a sneaky snaggle-toothed scoundrel leaving us to look like *schnooks*!"

"Schnooks?" asked Perce.

Rufuss rumbled, "Fools...dupes...*stupes*!"

Rufuss smiled a confident grin, and giggled out a simply grumpy song:

"It's just that kind of day,
When the schnooks are being sneaky!
Oh, there'll be a price to pay.
And I'll be there to say,
I told you so!

Now, we have to *go*.

I'm just too darn smart.
So, don't even start!

I am no ordinary rat.
To be rooked by any ordinary schnook!
A cunning rat
Can out-rook *any* such sneaky schnook.

Why, to put it quite plainly;
There is *no* rat
As ingenious,
As *stupendous,*
As super-smartious

As me!"

12

"Well, what do you think about *that* Perce?" asked the rat.

"Oh, rats!" Perce sighed, "I dropped my cookie."

Rufuss gasped, "*Rats?*" He wiped his face with his fingers in frustration. "Please, pay attention Perce. This is *important.*"

"Oh, Rufuss, *relax* and sit down," Perce replied, "That boy just wants to help. He's nothing so terrible as to be a little sneak. If he can stop that awful storm then, I'm all for it."

Rufuss insisted, "No, *no*. I'm telling you, we *must* leave the field before the storm floods us right out!"

Perce laughed and shook her head. "Now Rufuss, there is no sense getting all upset."

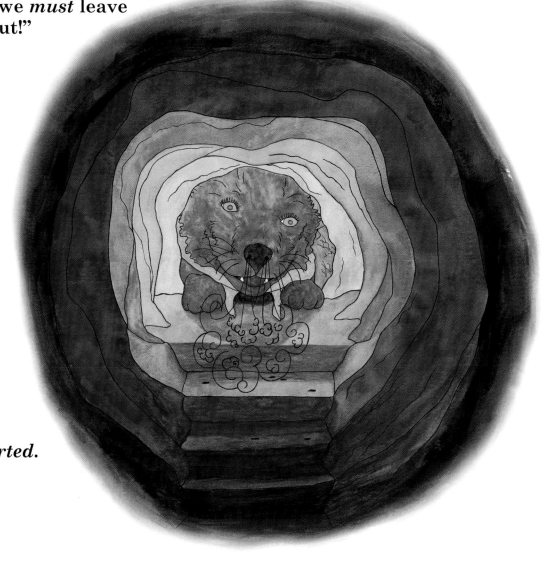

As Rufuss continued to grow louder with each word that he spoke, a large snouted nose protruded down the tunnel that lead to the rat's burrow.

It sniffed, and it *snorted.*

"Snoof!"

"Snort!"

13

"Snoof----sniff!"

The snoofing and snorting of the nose was so loud and so strong, that it blew the hairs on the animals heads back and forth. The rat's books flew off of their shelf, and the dusty dirt blew into a tiny twister...right there in his tunnel.

"Whoow...whooof...whooo...who's down there?" asked the nose.

At this, Rufuss grew very agitated. He marched straight up the tunnel, as he said to himself, "Just what creature would be so rude, that he would *snoof* and *snort* into my burrow without *first* introducing himself."

Rufuss placed his back against the intruder and *pushed*. He pushed hard on the large nose trying desperately to force it from his tunnel. The rat grunted and groaned, "Gha....grrr...ugh......uh...eeeehh!"

Finally, Rufuss was so tired from pushing and struggling with the nose that he gasped, and pleaded, "*Please*, whomever you are...why don't you just leave me *alone*?"

Suddenly, and without a sound, the nose pulled away from the hole in the ground. Rufuss quickly followed it to the surface; while Perce shivered in fear nervously hiding behind the rat.

14

"Be careful, Rufuss! You don't know what sort of scary monster it could be!" Perce warned.

Rufuss shrugged his shoulders and grunted, "*I don't care* if it's scary, or hairy, or...or even if its name is *Larry*! Whomever or whatever, I'm going to give it a piece of my mind!"

This long snouted nose actually belonged to a young coyote named Coogle. He was a fiery coyote, full of curiosity.

Rufuss cried out, "Oh, I might have known it would be *you* Coyote! Bumbling about *again*? *That* is all you ever do."

Coogle laughed, "How do, Old Pal! It's good to see ya." Coogle stood there with a mischievous grin. "Hey, was that *you* making so much noise?" laughed Coogle, "It sounded like ya tripped over a goat or somethin'. Are ya ok?"

Rufuss wiggled his nose and roared, "Of course it was me Coyote! Whooo else lives in myyyy burrow?" He thumped his fist into the palm of his hand and squealed, "Aaaand another thing, I'm quite capable of looking after myself...thank you!"

Coogle grinned and politely said, "How do, Miss Perce? It sure is a *fine* day."

Perce giggled. "It most certainly is Coogle."

Coogle's tongue hung out of his mouth while panting and slobbering all over the ground, and all over Rufuss.

"Put that tongue back in your mouth," hissed the rat, "You are dripping your doggy drool all over me!"

"Dag-nabbit!" steamed the rat, "What are you howling about Coyote?"
Brushing the dusty dirt from his fur, Rufuss began
to calm himself. "Well, as long as you are here
Coogle, you might as well know..."

"Know what?" asked Coogle, eagerly wagging his tail.

"There is a storm coming...more fierce
than *any* we have ever seen," exclaimed Rufuss.

Coogle's long ears sprang up to attention.
He howled, "*Jumpin'- jellyfish*, no foolin' Rufuss...
really for *true*?"

Rufuss squealed, "Yes, *yes*, really for true!
Why must you question *everything*, Coogle?
We have no time to babble. We must warn
the others before it is *too* late."

Coogle snickered, "Ok, *ok*, Rufuss, Old Pal."

In a stuffy manner, Rufuss scolded Coogle. "Old *Pal*!?
I told you *never* to call me that. My name is Rufussial T. Ratootious,
and I *expect* you to call me that."

Perce asked, "Why is there a 'T' standing in the middle of your name Rufuss?"
"If you must know, 'T' is for *Toot*," Rufuss replied, "Toot is my middle name."

"Toot? Ghah hoohee ha...then...then, I'll just call ya Toot!" laughed Coogle,
"That suits ya just fine."

Rufuss squeazed the top of his head with his hands.
"Oh, *I* give up," he muttered, "Let's just go."

With Coogle and Perce still laughing,
they scurried off to warn the other animals
of the coming storm.

Chapter 3
Pablo's Party

Meanwhile, on the other side of Color Field, the sounds of laughter and chatter barked loudly across the field of flowers and tall grass. Tiff, a young bobcat; her best friend, Tuttle, a field mouse, and a playful prairie dog named Albert, were having a party to welcome someone new, Señor Pablo P. Porcupine.

They blew on their party favors and cheered. "Hooray! Hooray for Pablo!"

Pablo was overcome with joy. He gasped, "What a splendid party. Such goodness I have *never* seen, not *anywhere* I have ever been."

"Have some strawberry pie, Pablo. I made it myself," touted Albert, while trying to muffle a burp.

Unknown to the others, Albert had already eaten most of the pie. He sat there grinning. He was stuffed to the brim with crumbs all over his chin.

"*Hey*, what's up here? There's no pie left for us!" cried Tuttle.

Albert tried to stop laughing, but that just made him laugh more.

"How could you, Albert? That pie was for Pablo," snapped the mouse, "I *never* saw such an eater in *all* my life."

"Except for Mrs. Moose!" laughed the cat.

Albert giggled, "My pie was delicious!"

"Well, now, that's *alright* Albert. Certainly, there is plenty left to share," said Pablo. "...And besides, I have found that there is no better sign of a great cook, than for him to eat *all* of what he has cooked." Pablo continued on saying, "I would be more than happy just to taste a little tidbit of this *delicious* masterpiece of cookery."

Albert snorkeled, "Ha haa...that's good! A little tidbit is about all there is left!" He fell backwards to the ground laughing uncontrollably.

All of the animals snickered and snorkeled, as each took a taste of what remained of the pie.
Tiff wiped her forehead and began to lick her paws clean. "It sure is hot today," she purred.

"If that sun gets any bigger, I'm gonna' fry like an egg," cried Tuttle.

"Mmmm...eggs are yummy," moaned Albert.
Tuttle hopped up and spouted, "Let's go swimming at Beaver's Pond!"

Albert cried out, "Oh, boy, I *like* Bernie. He knows more about mud and sticks than *anyone*."

"That buzzard?" Tiff groaned, "Beaver is always too busy chewing on sticks to have any fun."

Tuttle reasoned, "He just has too much work to do, Tiff. If we help Bernie with his work, then we can *all* go swimming."

"Splendid!" gasped Pablo. "I'm looking forward to meeting this Mr. Beaver."
"Perhaps, we should bring him a balloon from our party," suggested Pablo.

Tuttle replied, "Bernie can use it to float around on his belly *all* day."
"Now that's fun!" meowed the cat.

"Do ya think Bernie would mind if I chewed on some logs?" asked Albert.

"Are you nuts?" laughed Tiff, "Why do *you* want to chew on a *log*?"

Albert thought, "Gosh, *I* don't know...but if Bernie likes them so much, they must be *yummy*."

"You little pig...he's a *beaver*," Tiff laughed, "It's his job to chew on logs, as *crazy* as that is. That's what beavers do. Honestly, I think you'd eat just about *anything*, Albert."

"Golly, but I'm hungry?" said Albert.

"You're always hungry!" giggled Tuttle, "Albert is the 'bottomless belly'. We better stand clear of his mouth, or he just might eat us too."

The friends laughed and took their party with them. They were off to Beaver's Pond for a swim.

Chapter 4
Flupi-Ploop?

Along the path, butterflies of so many colors flickered and floated in the sunlight. One landed on Tuttle's head.

"Heewww, hallooo!" sighed the butterfly. "My wings are *so* sore. All that flapping... it's all day long!"

"That's a lot of flapping," remarked Pablo, "You must be pooped!"

Albert whispered into Tuttle's ear. Tuttle's eyes twinkled, and his tiny nose twitched as he listened. "Say, can you teach us to fly like you?" asked the mouse.

Mrs. Butterfly leaned forward with a great big smile. She looked a long look into Tuttle's beady little eyes. "You will have to learn how to do a flupi-ploop," she replied.

"A flupi-ploop...what's that?" asked Albert.

With listening ears and eyes all afire, the animals awaited her reply.

28

To all of their delight, the butterfly began
to flap her wings and sing:

"First...you...flap-flap *flop*!
And flutter flicker flutter...

With a flupi-ploop!
That's a very special swoop!

And you'll be on your way...
to a wonderful day!

Spending all of your time...
Floating the hours away!
Way up in the trees!

Grinning in the sunshine...
Flying with the *breeze*.

So, while you're flappin' with a flutter...
Say hello to Mr. Bee!
Because, you'll be flying like me...
When you go *flupi*-ploop!"

With such delightfulness, the animals began to sing. They flapped their arms. They
hopped about. They giggled, twisted, and twirled!

Pablo declared, "I have been most places, and I have seen many faces. I say, I've never seen anyone or...or *anything* as marvelous to see as *you* Mrs. Butterfly."

"Yer pretty," added Albert.

"Well, you're quite pretty yourself," said Mrs. Butterfly. "Have a wondrous day!" she shouted. Mrs. Butterfly waved goodbye and floated away.

"She said, I'm pretty!" boasted Albert, "No one *ever* said that to *me* before."

Tiff laughed, "That's because you're not a little girl...just a goofball!"

Tuttle pulled a dirty old string from out of his pocket and handed it to Albert. "Here!" he giggled, "Pretend *this* is a pretty pink ribbon. Now, if you tie it on top of your head, you can be as pretty as your sister, Perce."

Albert grinned and barked, "I'm not puttin' that stupid ol' string on *my* head!"

31

The cat and mouse laughed so much that they fell on the ground.

They could not even speak. They just laughed and laughed... "You stop that, or I'll stomp ya!" howled Albert.

All this rumpus began to rattle the bees that were buzzing about, and they came swarming after them.

Chapter 5
Get Running!

On the North end of the Field, Jesse and Kraukey hurried to reach the highest hilltop. Through tall grass, around a bend and over a hill, the pebbled path took them past a rusty wired fence.

Out of nowhere, a tremendous gust of wind lifted Kraukey from Jesse's head and slammed him into the fence. "Ahhwooooott!" he screeched.

Jesse ran after him shouting, "Oh, CREEPERS! Kraukey, are you ok?"

Kraukey stuttered as he struggled to untangle himself. "Ye...yes, I...I think so, but my....my wings are *stuck*. Ooooh, this is a d...dd...dilly of a pickle!"

Jesse helped Kraukey from the fence and placed him on the ground. The bird wiggled and wobbled as he staggered around. "I'm *so* dizzy ... I don't know if I'm comin' or goin'!" crowed Kraukey.

Jesse insisted, "I think you are going *home*, Kraukey Bird. You're not safe out here."

The little bird wiped his tears, sniffed, and squeaked. "Don't worry about me, boy. I'm a lot tougher than you think!"

"Yes, but still!" Jesse demanded, "We *have* to get you to a safe place."

Jesse took the bird back to his tree and said goodbye. "Believe in yourself, as *I* do," said the bird, "And hurry, you'd better get running!"

Jesse ran faster than ever before.

Chapter 6
A Buzzard of a Beaver

Back with Pablo's Party, the animals approached Beaver's pond. With the breezes blowing much stronger now, they were bullied by the wind.

Little did they know, but the strong winds that swished and swirled around them were the beginnings of the coming storm. Yet, the sun shined, and their thoughts were on other things.

Near the edge of the pond, they heard loud chomping and chewing. The sounds leaped off of the water and bounced off of the trees.

"Chomp!

Chew---chew!

Chomp!"

The strange noises led them to Bernie Beaver. Bernie's coat shimmered with wetness, as he gnawed his way through the bark of a tree.

"Howdy, Bernie! That's a mighty big tooth-pick!" laughed Tuttle.

"Tooth-pick? This is a *tree*," gargled Bernie.
Then he chuckled, "Ah, ho-ho, I see...very funny Mr. Mouse, *very* funny."

Albert snorkeled, "Hey, Bernie, what's that funny lookin' thing on yer head?"

Bernie cringed at the sound of Albert's voice and snarled, "Why, you puddin' head! This ain't just some funny lookin' thing. *This* is my swimmin' cap."

"Can't ya swim without yer cap?" asked Albert.

"Yes, *I* can swim without my cap," Beaver grumbled.

"Gee whiz, then, what's it on yer head fer?" laughed Albert.

Bernie bellowed, "To keep my head from gettin' all soggy you silly!"

Albert began to ask another question when Bernie stopped him. "Confound it! Can't you see how busy I am? What do all of you want?"

Albert started to shake and stutter. "We...weee...all came ...tt...to see if..."

"I told you...Bernie is an old buzzard!" Tiff growled. The cat stuck her tongue out at Beaver and folded her arms to pout.

Bernie leaned back on his tail while nibbling on a stick, as if it were a delicious tasting ear of corn. "State your business. I'm losin' my patience," he poohed.

"I didn't know you had *any* to lose," laughed the cat.

"Beaver, don't be so grumpy. We came to help you with your work," explained Tuttle.
Tiff snarled, "Yea, don't be such an old stinky!"

40

Bernie stopped chewing. He spit out a piece of wood to say, "You...all of you...you want to help *me* with my work? That's very nice, but shouldn't all of you be gettin' ready for the storm?"

"Whah...uh...what storm?" asked Tuttle.

"Kraukey did not tell you? A terrible storm is blowin' this way!" cried Bernie. "It's goin' to destroy everthin' in its path...unless we can stop it."

"Stop *it*...but how?" shrieked Albert.

Bernie chuckled, "Huh hoo...crazy Kraukey thinks Jesse can stop the storm for us. How is a *boy* suppose to do that? Why, those two are already headed into that awful mess."

"Good heavens!" exclaimed Pablo. "We have to think about what we should do."

Bernie replied, "As far as *I'm* concerned, it's already been thunk! I'm goin' to finish my work. My dam needs more mud and more sticks, or the storm will simply blow it away!"

Hearing this, Tiff's back curled up and her eyes bulged out. "Why, you old buzzard. You're being very selfish!" roared Tiff.

"Yea, it's not nice just thinking about your *own* self, Beaver. We should try to help Kraukey and the boy," insisted Tuttle.

Beaver quickly babbled, as if to choke on his own words. "We...well...I...I guess..." He squirmed and wiggled like a worm on a hook. *"Ooooh,* all right! Maybe, we should help," Bernie grumbled.

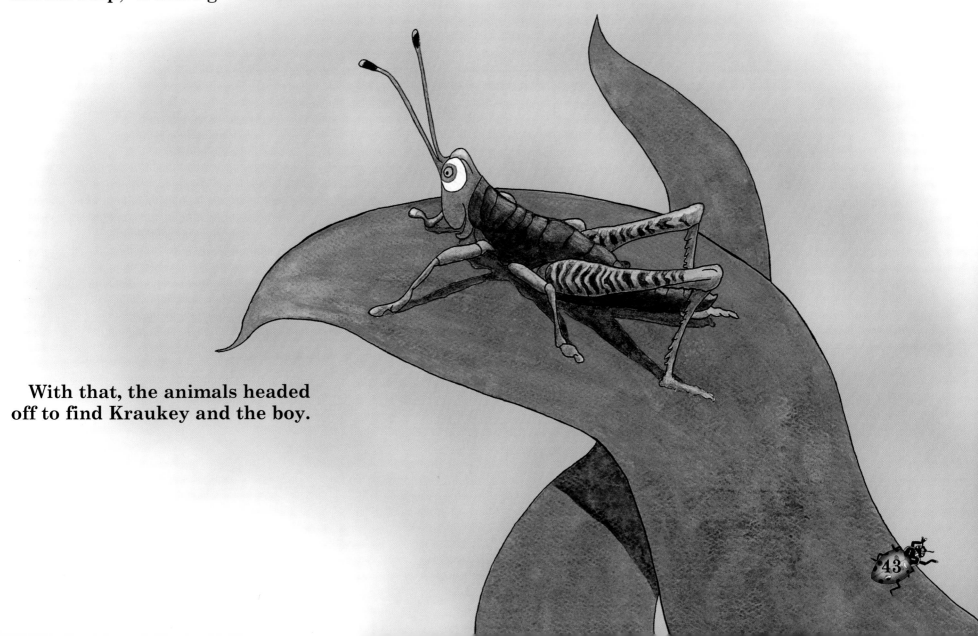

With that, the animals headed off to find Kraukey and the boy.

Chapter 7
The Big Wind Blew

But the cat was much too concerned to wait for the others. She ran far ahead of them. Soon she could see the boy running in the distance.

Huffing and puffing for air, Tiff cried out, "Je...Jesse, wait for me!" She ran straight up to him and screeched to a stop.

"Talking birds, talking cats... Now, I've heard everything!" exclaimed the boy. "Who are *you*?" he asked, "And how do you know who *I* am?"

Tiff was still trying to catch her breath.
"Hah...my...I'm Tiff," she gasped. "*Everyone* knows who you are, Jesse. We hide in the grass and watch you play."

Jesse smiled as he listened.

"Only yesterday, I saw you hopping around like a *frog*. What a silly!" laughed Tiff. "And then, you got *all* muddy rolling in the dirt. I bet your mom got *really* mad at you!"

Jesse snorkeled, "I was just pretending to be a Coyote."

"Now I know why you were so silly!" the cat replied, "That's the only way those goofs know how to be." Tiff's smile turned upside down. "Jesse, can you save Color Field from the storm...truly?"

The boy sighed, "Auwww, shucks... I'll try Tiff, but I don't know if I can."

"If Kraukey thinks you can, then I'm *sure* of it. That bird is a lot smarter than he looks," said the cat.

All of a sudden, there was a hooting and hollering from over the hill.

It was Kraukey, frantically flapping. He wrestled against the wind that tried to push him back down to the ground. The wind *cracked,* and Kraukey sputtered to his landing with a tumble and *crash.*

"Ahoohooheee!" he screeched.

Jesse scolded, "Kraukey, what are you doing here?"

Kraukey's eyes spun around in his head as he lifted his beak from the dirt. "I have no idea!" chirped the bird.

As they spoke, something slithered from behind the grass. It was Coogle Coyote. He picked up a dried out gourd with nothing left inside but seeds. Holding the gourd in his tail, Coogle shook it to make a rattling sound. And he began to hiss like a snake. "Ssszzz... sasah...sszzz...sasah..."

"Leapin' lizards!" shouted Jesse. "Did you hear *that*?"

The others froze with fright as Coogle leaped from the grass. "Bowooo! Bowooo!" he barked.

Tiff and Jesse tumbled backwards.

Before Kraukey could lift himself from the dirt, Coogle began sniffing the bird. He blew the dirt from Kraukey's feathers with a *snort*. "Hee ha!" laughed the coyote. "Scared ya! You thought *I* was a snake," he shouted.

"Phooey!" snapped Tiff. She turned her head away and snarled, "You *are* a snake." Tiff grabbed the gourd from Coogle's tail and growled. "Gimme' that you silly-sack!"

Coogle gave Kraukey Bird a friendly pat on the back. "How do, Kraukey!" Coogle said smiling.

His pat on the back made even more dirt fly out of Kraukey's feathery sleeves. The poor bird started to cough and sneeze. "Cauwkkk! Aaaah-choooo!"

"For heaven's sake, Coogle, what are you trying to *do* to me?" yelled Kraukey. "Today, I was blown from the sky, *thrown* into a fence, *burned* by lightnin', and now *you're* gonna' finish me off!"

Coogle howled, "Hoohee ha...Kraukey, you are *so* funny."

Suddenly, Coogle began to race around in circles chasing his tail with his teeth... for no reason at all.

He stopped just as quickly as he had started and stuck his nose out to sniff. "Snoof! Sniff...snort! You must be Jesse," said the silly coyote.

Jesse giggled, "You're the funniest looking snake that *I've* ever seen." As he pet Coogle, a flash of light appeared in the sky.

"Jumpin'-Jellyfish!" barked Coogle. "What was that?"

"Oh, creepers!" blurted Jesse, "We have to hurry!"

They were at the highest hilltop, and together they ran.
They leaped over tall grass and weeds. Jesse looked down to his side.
Barking and howling, Coogle Coyote was running stride for stride.
But as they ran up the hill, the big wind blew. Tiff and Coogle,
each took a tumbling spill.

The great wind picked up Kraukey,
and threw him into the distant trees.
"Here I go agaaaaain!" wailed the bird.

The animals were tossed like toys.

"ROWOOOO!" went the cat.

50

"HARROOOO!" howled the coyote.

Determined to save his friends, the boy ran on.
"Please, Mr. Cloud, stop your storm! Oh, please, listen to me!" he shouted.

With a flash of light the largest cloud swooped down to the hilltop;
and with a great burst of wind and rain from its mouth, the giant cloud
spoke with a rumble to the ground.
"JESSE, DO YOU KNOW WHAT YOU ASK?"

Jesse was frightened and fell to his knees.
"Aaaaaah! You're for real!" screamed the boy.

The cloud spit out its words.
"YOU MUST LISTEN JESSE! WITHOUT MY RAIN, THERE WOULD BE NO FIELD
FOR THE ANIMALS TO LIVE. AND THERE WOULD BE NO TREES FOR KRAUKEY
AND THE OTHER BIRDS TO MAKE THEIR HOMES."

"*Goodness,* where would they go?" cried Jesse.

The cloud swirled with lightning in its eye. Once again, it thundered.
"AND BOY, THERE WOULD BE NO WATER FOR BEAVER AND THE OTHERS TO
PLAY IN, OR TO DRINK. WHAT GOOD WOULD COME OF THAT?" asked the cloud.

Jesse just stood there up on the hill.
He could not believe what his eyes
were seeing, or his ears were hearing.

Yet, he knew. He knew that this must
be true.

The mighty cloud smiled and said, "DON'T YOU SEE, JESSE? MY STORM IS MUCH NEEDED HERE. BELIEVE ME BOY...YOU HAVE NOTHING TO FEAR."
"THIS PROMISE I'LL GIVE TO YOU: THE SKY WILL AGAIN SHINE BRIGHTLY, AND THE WIND WILL DIE DOWN LOW. BUT FOR NOW, MY STORM MUST BLOW."

Shaking the ground with his voice, the cloud burst, "GO QUICKLY NOW, LITTLE ONE. YOU MUST FIND COVER, FOR IT IS TIME!"

The wind blew hard. The large storm cloud rushed forward, and then upward to the sky. With a tremendous *CRASH* and *KA-BOOM*, the storm began.

Chapter 8
A Friend to Keep

Jesse and the animals hurried for cover in the dark woods. They huddled together to stay warm and dry beneath the branches of a large tree. With lightning flashing and thunder thumping, a heavy rain fell.
The lightning crackled across the sky creating strange shadows and frightful images through the forest trees.

"It is ss...so spooky in here!" Tiff shuttered. "I th...th...think I see something looking at us ff...ff...from behind that t...tt...tree over there," she cried.

Kraukey trembled. "Mah...Maybe, it's a mo...monster!"
Coogle barked loudly. He tried his best to scare whatever it was away. Finally, the coyote laughed out, "There's nothin' behind that tree, except another tree!"

Kraukey covered his eyes with his wings and moaned. "It's more than dark in these woods... it's spooky!"

"Gee, you critters don't have to be afraid," Jesse said, "All you have to do is think about candy canes and hot dogs. It *always* works for me."

Kraukey shuttered, "Ca...Ca...Candy canes, and ho...ho...hot dogs?"

"All I can thah...think about are Gooblioos!" whined Tiff, "I bet they're all around us...creepin' up on every side of us."

"Wha...whah.... What's a Gooblioo?" screeched Kraukey.

56

Tiff shivered. "*Oh*, they're a gooey mess! A Gooblioo is like a big clump of melting ice cream, with a super long banana nose. And you know...a nose like that can sniff you out of *wherever* you're hiding," she explained.

Jesse grimaced and groaned, "Auwww...*Tiff*, why did you have to go and tell us *that*? How can I *ever* eat another ice-cream cone?"

57

"Yea, what silly slop are you fillin' our heads with?" Kraukey crowed.

"Well, it's *true*," meowed Tiff.
"And they've got heads like whipped cream with big cherries on top.....*oooh*, and...and long goopey arms to catch you with!"

Still hiding under his wings, Kraukey moaned, "I don't want to hear any more!"

"Are the wittle babies scared o' Tiff's ice cream clumps?" Coogle teased.
"WAAAH! Heehee-hah!" he laughed and pointed at Tiff.

Tiff shouted, "Look-out behind you, Coogle, it's a Gooblioo!"

Coogle sprang all the way up the tree screaming as he went, "YEEEEEEOW!"

Tiff snorkeled and slapped her knee. "What a maroon! That was just your *tail* Coyote. I'll teach you to make fun of *me*," she giggled.

"Go ahead...laugh!" barked Coogle, "I'm *not* comin' down."

58

Kraukey pleaded with him. "Coogle, get down. It's very slick and swirly up there. You might slip and fall!"

"Nope! I like this tree. Maybe, I'll even become a *bird*," laughed Coogle.

Kraukey shrieked, "A bird! You must be gettin' dizzy up there Coyote."

"All that rain must have washed away his brain," Tiff snorkeled.

"K-KRACKLE!" A streak of lightning struck the top of Coogle's tree and split it in two.

"AUUUGHH!" howled Coogle.

"Kirplunk!" He plopped on the ground like a sack of potatoes. "Oh, my *aching* head," croaked Coogle.

Tiff laughed out, "Look! A nut fell out of the tree!"

The rain stopped. One by one, they peered and popped out from the woods. What they saw was a colorful rainbow. It stretched farther than anyone could see.

"WOW!" roared Tiff.

Kraukey chirped, "It's simply wonderful!"

"I wonder where it goes to," barked Coogle.

There were sparkles in Jesse's eyes as he said, "It's never ending... It goes on and on, forever and *ever*."

The end of the storm had finally come. The rest of the animals met Jesse, Kraukey, Tiff, and Coogle along the muddy path. The animals cheered for Jesse. They thanked him for being such a good friend.

Jesse looked down at the ground and scuffed at the dirt with his foot. "But, I could not stop the storm from coming," he said. "It came! I could do *nothing*," cried Jesse.

Pablo stepped forward to say, "Yes, but you did *all* that you could *do*. And that's more than most others would even *think* of doing."

"Jesse, *you* are a true friend," Coogle said smiling.

Rufuss declared, "You see Perce...*I* told you... He's a very fine boy."

"Oh, really?" laughed Perce, "I thought you called him a sneeky schnook."

Pablo chuckled and extended his prickly paw to shake Jesse's hand. But the boy abruptly jumped back. "OUCH! You poked my finger," he cried.

"Oh, dear, I'm just too prickly for my own good," Pablo explained.

Albert laughed, "Hooo-hee...and much too prickly for Jesse's good too!"

Pablo chuckled, cleared his throat, and sang a little song.

"I have prickly toes,
Even *thorns* on my *nose*.
But, well, when you're a porcupine...
That is the way it should be.

When I put on my hat
I poke holes in *that*.

And, when I sit on a stinky something
So very stinky,
It always seems to resemble
Some sort of *smelly* swiss cheese!

Oh, can you imagine
How it is to be...
Pablo P. Porcupine?

When I fall on my fanny,
I find it hard to stand up
Without a good friend or two.

It's one simple fact
That sticks to me...

I'm Pablo P. Porcupine!"

Everyone laughed and jumped in puddles to play, for they knew all was ok.
And just as the storm cloud had promised: The sky shined brightly, and the
wind died down low. The friends had weathered the storm together. They walked along the
muddy path splashing wherever they could.

"Whoopi!" yelled Jesse, with a splash of his feet.

"I guess rainy days aren't so bad after all," he said smiling, "That was the *bestest*
time ever."

The afternoon sun began to stretch and yawn above the clouds.
Jesse said goodbye to his new friends. He returned to the old gray fence beneath the
tall timber trees of Color Field. There, he laid down to rest and stared at the sky above.

"It was *so* great to see you today, Mr. Cloud."

Jesse could hear his mother calling for him in the distance. Her voice floated across
the field rolling right over him. "Jesse! Jesse, it's time to come home!"

But Jesse still wanted to play. His happy face turned to a frown.

Yet, suddenly, he smiled and laughed out, "What fun! I can't wait to come
back tomorrow!"

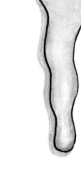
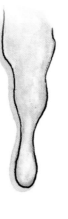
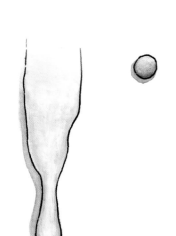

The
End

Jesse's Color Field
Copyright 2002 by S.K. Miller
All rights reserved.
Published by Treehouse Treasures Corporation.
Jesse, Kraukey, Coogle, Tiff, Tuttle, Albert, Bernie, Rufuss, Pablo P. Porcupine, Perce, the Gooblioos, Mrs. Butterfly,
and all related characters are trademarks of Treehouse Treasures Corporation.

No part of this publication may be reproduced in whole or in part, or stored in a retrieval system, or transmitted in any form or
by any means, electronic, mechanical, photocopying, recording, or otherwise, without the written permission of S.K. Miller.

For information regarding permission, write to Treehouse Treasures Corporation, P.O. Box 1030, St. Charles, Illinois, 60174.

~~~~~~~~

Library of Congress Cataloging-in-publication Data
Miller, S.K.
Summary: A young boy is confronted by a terrible storm.
While trying to save the animals of Color Field, he learns what friendship and caring are all about.
LOC# 2001119863
ISBN 0-9714636-0-3

{1. Animals--Fiction. 2. Boy--Fiction. 3. Storm--Fiction.}

Printed in Spain BY MONDADORI.

To my Father in heaven, I love you and thank you!

To Jeannie, Sean, Jesse, Stevie, and my entire family, you are wonderful!
Without all of your love and support, this book would not be.

To mom, a special thanks for your giving heart and the many stories.

Thanks to Paula and Prographics.

15% of profits will be donated to Children In Need.